THE TOP SECRET DIARIES OF TWIN SISTERS

TWINNING

**To the real Ms Phillips—
Elizabeth! A.M.**

Scholastic Australia
An imprint of Scholastic Australia Pty Limited
PO Box 579 Gosford NSW 2250
ABN 11 000 614 577
www.scholastic.com.au

Part of the Scholastic Group
Sydney • Auckland • New York • Toronto • London • Mexico City
New Delhi • Hong Kong • Buenos Aires • Puerto Rico

Published by Scholastic Australia in 2024.

Series design by Sofya Karmazina.

NATIONAL LIBRARY OF AUSTRALIA
A catalogue record for this book is available from the National Library of Australia

ISBN: 978-1-76129-339-9

Typeset in KG First Time In Forever, Schoolbell Pro, DK Harimau Dua, Pacific Northwest, Esmeralda, Trash Hand, Margarine.

Printed in China by Hang Tai Printing Company Limited. This product is made of material from well-managed FSC®-certified forests, recycled materials, and other controlled sources.

FSC www.fsc.org
MIX
Paper | Supporting responsible forestry
FSC® C023121

10 9 8 7 6 5 4 3 2 1　　24 25 26 27 28 / 2

THE TOP SECRET DIARIES OF TWIN SISTERS

TWINNING

by ALEXA MOSES

SKIPPING STARS

Illustrated by SOFYA KARMAZINA

A Scholastic Australia Book

Izzy
Monday night

One day, someone will **DEFINITELY** turn this diary into a real book! After all, I'll be the greatest hip-hop star on the planet, so my fans will want to know **EVERYTHING** about me.

What does Izzy T like to eat, they'll ask?

Answer: Double-bacon burgers, red velvet cake and Fizz Missile **lollies**.

Does she really keep reptiles on her private jet?

Answer: Although snakes are awesome, the answer is **NO**. That would be too cruel.

Is she really an identical twin?

Answer: Yes, although Grace, my sister, is very different to me. She's more likely to become a **FASHION DESIGNER** working backstage, because she hates being in the spotlight.

And what does Izzy T like to do when she's not on stage wowing her fans?

Answer: Right now, it's **SKIPPING!**

I'm one of the **BEST SKIPPERS** at Rocky Point Primary. That sounds like I'm bragging, but hey, this is MY diary. It's also the back of my maths book, which means I'm **running out of space** for maths. I figure my fans need my deep thoughts more than my fractions homework.

Anyway, back to the good stuff—**SKIPPING!** Right now, all the Year 5 and 6 girls are into it. Every day, when the bell rings for break, we run to the shed for skipping ropes. The ropes everyone wants are the green ones, but there are only two of them. They're heavy and thick and slap the ground just right.

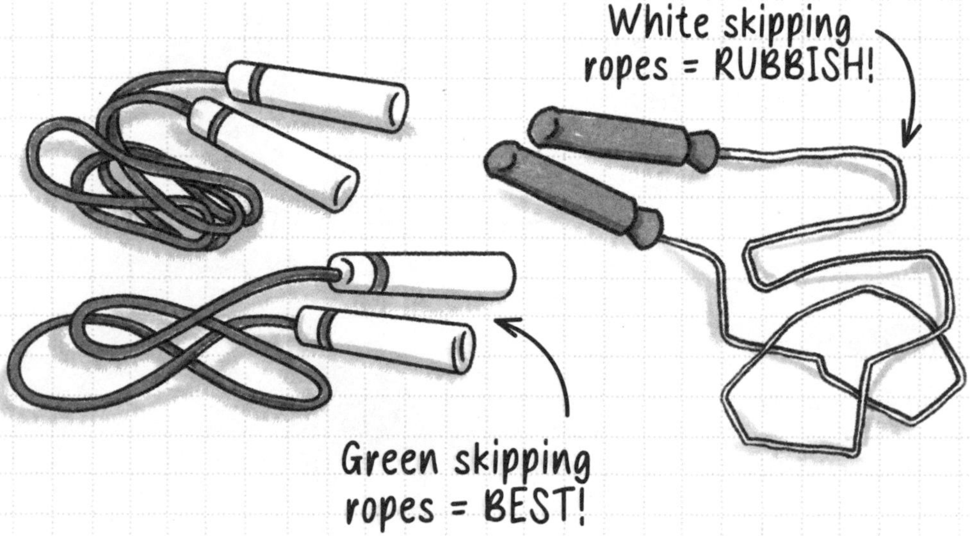

The only **BAD** thing about skipping is my group. They like skipping, but they're not serious about it. After fifteen minutes, they get tired and want to sit down like a bunch of old ladies. I spend more time begging my group to skip than I spend **actually skipping**. But how will they get better without practice?

'Izzy, I don't have time to practise after school today,' Sienna said.

I'd just shown her a hopping exercise to help her learn double-dutch. **DOUBLE-DUTCH** is where you skip with two ropes instead of one. Sienna and Grace can only skip with a single rope.

'Why not?' Otti asked.

'The Rocky Point Primary waste system is in **crisis!**' Sienna said. 'The kindy kids are throwing food scraps into the wrong bins. Who wants to help me sort it out?'

REALLY?! Sienna wanted us to sort rotting banana peels instead of *skip*? *She* was the Year 5 Environment Captain, not us!

'I've got homework,' Grace said quickly.

'I've got ballet practice,' Otti said.

'Are you kidding?' I said to Sienna. '**GROSS!**'

Why were we talking about rubbish when we could have been skipping? If I don't practise, I won't **stay** one of Rocky Point's best skippers.

Everyone knows who the best skippers on the playground are. Willow Yu, who's super nice, is third best. But first and second best are trickier. It's between me and—this hurts to write—**CLOVER WILLIAMS!**

Clover and I were friends last year, before she stole my squishy hamburger keyring. Since then, Clover and I have been **MORTAL ENEMIES!** And lunch today turned into an epic skip-off between us, because Clover Williams likes to be the best at **everything**.

Sienna was at a Student Council meeting (she is also our Year 5 Student Council Representative), so Otti and Grace were turning the ropes. Grace's eyes widened.

'Don't look, but Clover's watching,' she said.

So **of course**, I looked!

Clem and Harper were turning the green ropes so fast their hair blew up. Clover leapt in, did two half-turns and jumped out. She caught my eye and smiled.

What a show-off!

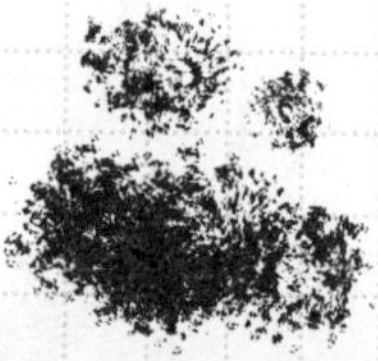

Lots of people believe twins can **READ EACH OTHER'S MINDS**, but that's rubbish. What we *can* do is talk to each other using our faces and bodies.

Grace's face said.

I responded, narrowing my eyes.

Grace's tiny shrug meant.

'Turn faster,' I told Otti and Grace.

I jumped in, did some **karate kicks** and ended with a breezy star jump out of the rope. *Take that, Clover Williams!*

Clover looked as if someone had karate-kicked her phone across a field.

Around the playground, ropes slowed and **handballs** stopped. Everyone was watching us.

Again, Clover leapt into her ropes, did sprints and heel taps . . . then **CARTWHEELED** out of the ropes!

As the playground burst into applause, Clover smiled. Double *hmmmph*.

'When I nod, slow the ropes, OK?' I said.

'Sure,' Otti nodded.

I was going to pull off a trick where the skipper drops into a **squat** and kicks forwards. It only works if the rope-turners slow down. If not, the skipper will trip.

I jumped in and skipped for a bit, then nodded. I crossed my arms and squatted . . . but Grace and Otti kept whipping the ropes around!

'**SLOW DOWN!**' I yelled, but it was too late. I lost my balance and **SMACKED** backwards onto the concrete.

Everyone watching winced.

'Ouch,' someone said loudly.

Exactly. My **butt** was sore and my chin stung where one of the ropes had slapped me. Still, my pride hurt worse, especially when Clover high-fived her friends. **UGH!**

Across the playground, ropes started turning and handballs bouncing again. The skipping battle was **over**, and I'd lost. Badly.

'Why didn't you slow down?' I asked my friends.

'You didn't nod,' Otti said.

'I did! Grace?'

'Sorry, I was looking at the sky,' Grace said, pointing to a bunch of puffy clouds. 'The clouds are like **MOUNTAINS** today. Are you OK?'

I sighed. Why does my twin care more about *clouds* than skipping?

'I'm fine,' I said.

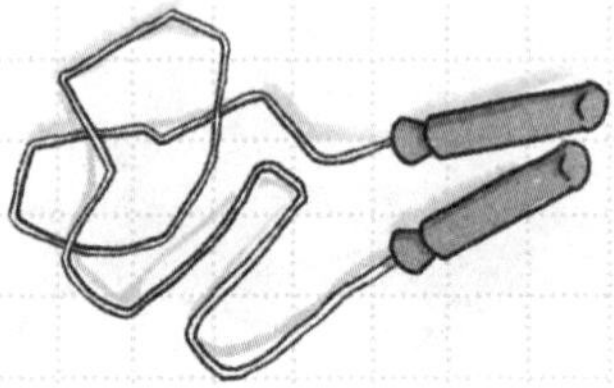

'Why don't you take a break?' Grace suggested. She offered me the ropes. 'Want to turn? Otti and I haven't skipped yet.'

COME ON! Grace had tripped me up and now she was taking away my practice time?! If I don't practise, Clover will be the Rocky Point Skipping **GOAT** instead of me! (**GOAT** means Greatest of All Time, future fans. Try to keep up).

I shot Grace a look that said, *You're kidding.*

Nope, Grace's twitch of the rope meant. When Grace makes up her mind, she's like an enormous rock—she won't budge.

So, I turned the ropes. Otti was **worried** about hurting her feet before her ballet exam, so she made us turn super slow. Turning is so dull . . . zzzzzz.

Of course, Clover's friends turned the ropes all recess so Clover could practise. Clover did trick after trick and didn't turn **at all**.

At last, the bell rang, ending my torture.

Assembly was the usual blah, blah, blah from our principal, Crome Dome. Clover was sitting in my row. I could **FEEL** her being smug, like heat blasting off a fire.

When I tuned back in, Crome Dome was saying, 'I have some exciting news, RPP. Our school has been chosen to feature in a **SPECIAL VIDEO** to promote schools in our area. A TV crew from the Department of Education will visit us on Wednesday next week to film a normal day at RPP. Consent notes will be sent home today.'

A **buzz** ran through the crowd.

'The producer seemed especially keen to film our lunchtime skipping. Skippers, perhaps you'd like to form teams and put together short routines for the camera crew?'

The noise got deafening as everyone **FREAKED OUT!**

'RPP, let's take ten deep breaths!' Crome Dome called, clapping his hands.

My thoughts were bouncing around like **PING-PONG** balls. A TV crew was coming to Rocky Point Primary and they wanted to film the skipping! Surely, the best skippers would star in their footage?

Clover and I gave each other **hard stares**.

It was **ON!**

Grace

Tuesday, 8.22 p.m.,
before bed

Last year, the Library Monitors had to dust **every book** in the library.

I *loved* that job. The old books smelt like sun-baked soil, and their pages felt like dry silk. I even found a **VINTAGE** craft book with dress patterns for dolls. And our librarian, Ms Phillips, let me keep it!

Izzy would *hate* dusting books. She said even the thought of it was so **boring**, it made her want to throw a book out the window.

Well, how Izzy felt about the thought of dusting books is how *I* feel about skipping. It's soooooo boring, I want to toss the skipping ropes over the playground fence! But I haven't told Izzy the truth about how I feel. Right now, all the girls in our year are crazy about skipping, and Izzy's the **craziest** of all.

Last week, Soraya Savvas and Willow Yu got into a big argument over the lime-green ropes, which Izzy says are the best. Mr Crome gave us all a lecture and put a padlock on the shed door. He also picked a Skipping Captain to unlock the shed and hand out the ropes at recess.

He chose **CLEM CHAU**, who is one of Clover's best friends. Every break, she disappears into the office and comes out again carrying Mrs Allsop's enormous keyring.

(Mrs Allsop is the school secretary.) There must be twenty keys on it! Clem **marches** across the playground to the sports shed, jangling those keys all the way. I guess it makes her feel important.

Clem Chau, 10

- Clover's best friend
- Loves being in charge
- Skipping Captain
- Always has the latest fashion accessories

Sienna says Clem's gone into the teachers' toilet using those keys! I'd **love** to see inside the teachers' toilet! I bet it has gold taps, and fluffy white handtowels in a basket, and scented candles too.

'Lining up for ropes is a bit silly,' Otti said, as we **trudged** to the shed. 'Clem always gives her friends the best ropes.'

I nodded glumly.

Then, while we waited in line, I saw a Year 1 girl sitting under a tree with a shopping bag beside her. She was pulling purple packets from the bag, tearing each packet open and taking out TINY TOYS.

Scattered in the grass around her were the sweetest little unicorns and winged horses! All of them had big, sad eyes.

'What are those?' I asked, approaching her.

The girl frowned up at me like I was interrupting her.

'**FILLY FRIENDS**,' she said.

'They're **CUTE**,' I said. 'Where did you get them?'

'The supermarket,' she said. 'You get one for every twenty dollars you spend.'

I didn't like the way the girl was tossing those horses aside. They gazed at me like they were **begging me** to save them!

'Why are you throwing them away?' I asked.

The little girl took out another packet. On the packet were the words, '**Collect Them All**'.

'I'm looking for a Silver Alicorn,' she said. 'The Silver Alicorn is *really* rare. No-one at RPP has one.'

'What's an *alicorn*?' I asked.

She gazed at me with **scorn**.

'A unicorn is a horse with a horn,' she said slowly, as if I were a toddler. 'A **PEGASUS** is a horse with wings. And an alicorn has a horn *and* wings.'

'Could I have one of those, please?' I said, pointing to the toys in the grass.

The girl shrugged.

'OK. But only a **purple unicorn**,' she said. 'I've got lots of them.'

She **ripped** the last packet open and took out a purple unicorn.

'Rats,' she said, and passed it to me. It felt **smooth and cool** in my hand, and I rubbed my thumb over its horn.

I thanked her and hurried back to Otti, who'd got the worst ropes again.

As we walked across the playground, Izzy waved at us from beside the **FRIENDSHIP TREE**. Every day, Izzy saves her favourite skipping spot by pacing up and down and glaring at any kid who comes close, while we get the ropes.

Izzy shook her head when she saw the white ropes Otti held.

I raised my eyebrows, which meant, *Sorry, but there was* ***nothing*** *we could do.*

Otti plonked down under the Friendship Tree and opened her lunchbox.

'Come on, Otti, lunch is half over,' Izzy said. 'Sienna's at another **Student Council** meeting. I need you to turn the ropes!'

'But I'm hungry,' Otti moaned.

'Please?' Izzy said. 'Pretty please with **GUMMY WORMS** on top?'

'Alright,' Otti said, and shoved her sandwich into her mouth.

For once, as Otti and I turned, I wasn't thinking about **how boring skipping was**. I was thinking about the purple unicorn in my pocket, and how Filly Friends were so cute! I wanted to collect them all!

When I got home, I put my purple unicorn on the bookshelf beside my Sweet Sisters dolls.

No–one was at home except for my older sister, Elodie, who was in her room playing **TRUMPET**. I was alone!

When we were little, Izzy wasn't into dolls, so I played by myself, and I've done it ever since. It's really relaxing. Still, I'd hate **anyone** to know about it.

I bet **no-one** else in Year 5 still plays with dolls.

I made my smallest Sweet Sister doll feed the purple unicorn and groom her coat. They were about to go for a ride across my desk when Izzy **burst** into the room.

'What are you doing?' Izzy said, tossing her soccer boots into her **MESS PILE**.

The Mess Pile lives by Izzy's bed. Every few months, Mum makes Izzy clean it, but it always grows again. In the dark, it looks like a **creepy** monster! *Shudder.*

I shoved **everything** back on the bookshelf.

'Tidying my collection,' I said.

Izzy might be my twin, but even *she* doesn't know I still play with dolls sometimes.

Izzy **flopped** onto her bed to watch skipping videos on Mum's tablet, so I gave up on playing and used our laptop to look up Filly Friends.

There are six unicorns and six Pegasuses to collect. The thirteenth and **RAREST** Filly Friend is the Silver Alicorn. Every time I gazed into her alicorn eyes, I got this strong, wanty feeling.

Dinner tonight was burgers, which we all love. And when Dad lays out all the fillings, they look so pretty. He puts out juicy red tomato slices, crispy green lettuce and tangy brown onion rings that smell so good. As we made our burgers, Izzy talked about the Department of Education video.

'If I could nail a cartwheel out of the ropes, that would be **awesome**,' she said, helping herself to tomato sauce and bacon.

'Wow,' Dad said.

'Today I saw the cutest little things,' I said, putting a deep-pink slice of beetroot on my veggie burger. 'They're these MAGICAL HORSES called Filly Friends.'

'Oh, really?' Mum said.

'Cartwheels are **super hard**,' Izzy went on. 'The timing has to be just right.'

'Did you know that alicorns are flying unicorns?' I said. 'They're horses with wings *and* horns.'

Elodie put a slice of cheese on her burger.

'You're both **obsessed**,' she said.

Izzy and I glared at her.

'We are not!' we said, and picked up our burgers.

For a while, the only sounds were **munching** and **crunching** and happy little **sighs**.

'Dad,' I said, before Izzy started up about skipping again. 'Are you going shopping tomorrow?'

'Yep,' he said. 'What do you need?'

I took the purple unicorn from my pocket.

'These come with the SHOPPING at the supermarket,' I said. 'You get one for every twenty dollars you spend. Could you get me some, please?'

'Aww, so cute,' Dad said, making my unicorn walk across the table.

'Filly Friends are a **sneaky way** for the shops to make money,' Elodie said, as she reached for the salad bowl. 'Parents buy more than they need to get those toys for their children. Besides, I thought you'd **OUTGROWN** dolls, Grace.'

I felt like a plastic cup that had been stamped on.

'They're not *dolls,*' I said. 'They're **collectibles**. Collecting isn't babyish. Grown-ups collect things like coins and comics all the time.'

'Yeah, and who made you boss of the house, **Smelodie?**' Izzy said, and kicked Elodie under the table.

'Owwww!' Elodie said. 'Mum, tell her to stop!'

'Izzy, please don't kick your sister and don't call her that name,' Mum said, sighing.

'She deserves it,' Izzy said. 'Gee can play with dolls if she wants.' (Sometimes we still use our **TWIN LANGUAGE**, and *Gee* is twin for 'Grace'.)

Great, even Izzy thought I was a baby!

'I don't want to play with *dolls*,' I told her. '**I want to start a collection.**'

Mum put her hand on my shoulder.

'Sweetie, Elodie's got a point. Those unicorns are cute,

but they're a waste of money and they're not good for the **environment**, either. Can't you play with the dolls you already have?'

My family never *listens* to me!

'They're **not** dolls!' I said, but Izzy was talking about skipping again.

After dinner, it was my turn to stack the dishes. As I carried our plates into the kitchen, I was **HORRIBLY** sad. I felt like the colour the water goes when Izzy soaks her football socks in the laundry sink. Dismal Grey, that's what I felt.

Izzy thought I was a baby who played with dolls, *and* Mum had said no to Filly Friends. When Mum says no, **that's the end of it**.

Then Dad ducked into the kitchen.

'Don't worry about *them*,' he said, setting my purple unicorn on the counter.

I felt a tiny **flash** of hope.

'Who do you think does the grocery shopping in this house?' Dad went on.

YES!!!

Izzy

Wednesday, whenevs

You know how on Monday I thought it was **ON** with Clover Williams? Well, today, something **SUPER WEIRD** happened, but I need to go back to last night to explain.

After school, I came into our bedroom with Mum's tablet to watch skipping videos. I wanted Grace to watch, but she was reading about those horse dolls on our laptop.

I don't get why Grace loves those little horses! True, she's always been into dolls. I caught her playing with hers again yesterday, doing these squeaky voices. I pretend I don't know so she doesn't get embarrassed.

Anyway, I lay on the bed and watched these pro-skipper videos. They are **CRAZY** good! They do flips and even handstands in the ropes. My favourite trick is a leapfrog, where one skipper jumps over another. I wish my friends were good enough to do leapfrogs with me.

I was so inspired, I came up with a **FIERCE** skipping routine to do for the TV crew. Double-dutch, of course.

Izzy T's FIERCE Skipping Routine

1. Jump in and go straight into skiers, which are side-to-side bounces.

2. High karate kicks, where you leap up and kick one leg out straight in front, and then alternate with your other leg.

3. Teddy-bear bounces, where you squat down and touch the ground.

4. Tuck jumps, where you bring your knees up high to touch your chest.

5. And the big finish . . . CARTWHEEL out of the rope then land in the SPLITS!

I called it **ITFSR** for short. Awesome, right?

Grace and Sienna can turn the ropes. Otti can skip with me until the tuck jumps and then leap out, and I'll do the big finish without her. 'Cause even though Otti can cartwheel *and* do the splits, she doesn't want to hurt herself before her ballet exam.

ITFSR will be **AMAZING!** And once the Department of Education video goes viral, I'll **definitely** be asked to lead the national skipping team. I can totally be a professional skipper and a hip-hop star at the same time! The skipping team will just have to train on my private jet.

I decided that our group would have to practise **ITFSR** behind the Friendship Tree, because I didn't want anyone seeing the routine before the TV crew. Especially not anyone with a name that sounds like **DROVER SMILLIAMS**.

While we ate lunch today, I showed Sienna, Otti and Grace

how to do **ITFSR**, although it's hard to do tuck jumps while you're eating a sandwich.

'It has to be perfect,' I said. 'We only get one shot at it.'

But there was a problem, and her name started with S and ended with A. I knew Sienna was upset because her eyes had gone **SUPER** buggy.

'So, Grace and I would just turn the ropes while you and Otti skip?' Sienna asked. 'We wouldn't skip in the video at all?'

'Well, Otti and I *are* the best skippers,' I said carefully.

'That's right,' Otti said, but not in a **SHOW-OFFY** way. She said it like it was true. Which it is.

'And we want to give our best performance, since it will be on TV,' I said.

'It doesn't matter who's best,' Sienna said. 'We're a team, so we should all be equal.'

Sienna is **OBSESSED** with everyone being equal! If she had her way, she'd probably change our skipping routine so it had no hard tricks and we all jumped for the same amount of time. Sienna's routine would be **fair**. But it would also be **SO BORING** that the TV crew would fall asleep. *Zzzzzzz!*

'Good point, Sienna,' Grace said.

I couldn't believe Grace was on Sienna's side! I shot her a cranky look. *Who cares about* ***fair*** *when we're trying to be* ***great****, Gee?*

Grace's eyebrows twitched. *I care, Ziz,* her eyebrows said. *And you're turning the rope first today.* (Grace and I had a **SECRET TWIN LANGUAGE** when we were little, and *Ziz* is twin for 'Izzy'.)

I was about to answer when a face appeared around the Friendship Tree. It was **CLOVER WILLIAMS!**

We stared.

'Hi, guys,' Clover said. She seemed almost . . . nice?

'Excuse me?' I said, like **ICE**. I was so chilly, a penguin could have walked across me and not noticed I was a human girl.

'Look, Izzy, I know we've had . . . problems—' Clover started.

I snorted.

'You think?' I said.

'But I'm having trouble with that **trick** you did,' she said. 'The squat-bounce. I was wondering if you'd help me.'

Clover Williams was asking **ME** for help?

I glanced at my friends. Sienna was doing **BUG EYES** again, but at least it was at Clover instead of me.

'Why would I help you?' I asked.

'Because you're the best skipper on the playground,' Clover said.

Wow! **WOW!**

I still can't believe Clover said that! I KNOW she was probably just flattering me. I'm not dumb. Still, I think she secretly meant it.

'Could you show me, please?' Clover said. 'You can have a **quick skip** too. Harper and Clem are happy to turn the ropes.'

'Let me check with my team,' I said, trying to sound **PROFESH**.

While Clover waited by the sandpit, our group **huddled** under the Friendship Tree.

'She's using you to make their team look better for the Department of Education video,' Sienna said.

'It's only **one trick** and it's not in our routine,' Otti said. 'Does it matter?'

'If you showed her, Clover's crew would be grateful,' Grace added. 'They might be nicer to us.' Grace likes everyone to get along.

Sienna snorted like a **GRUMPY HORSE**.

'Are you saying we should *trust* Clover Williams?!' she said.

'Not with anything important,' Grace replied.

'I know what you mean, Sienna . . . but maybe Otti and Grace are right?' I said. 'It's just one trick.'

Sienna's lips were a **tight, thin line**.

'Do whatever you want,' she said.

So, here's the truth—I was **dying** to skip with Clover's group! First, they had the best green ropes. Second, Harper and Clem turned **FAST** and smooth, like they were whipping butter. And third, well . . . I wanted to skip with Clover because she was great at skipping. It's fun to skip with someone as good as me! Does that make me a **sneak**? Maybe, but it's not like I was hurting anyone!

And I was pretty sure Clover wanted to skip with me too. After all, she could have learnt the **SQUAT-BOUNCE** in ten minutes from an online video tutorial.

I waved to Clover.

'I'll help you with that *one* move,' I called.

As Clover and I walked across the playground, everyone **stared**. The whole school knew about the bust-up between us.

'Hi,' Clem said, and Harper nodded. Neither of them seemed to want me there, and I couldn't blame them. The situation was **TOTALLY** awkward. But they just started turning the ropes.

'Show me what you're doing,' I said.

Clover jumped in. She started to drop, but ended up on her hands and knees, the ropes getting **tangled** on her.

'You've got to drop quicker and really go for it,' I said. 'Watch.'

Like I said, Clem and Harper are **SUPER** rope-turners, so I skipped a little longer than I needed to before I showed Clover the trick.

'I see,' Clover said, and **jumped** in as I leapt out.

On her next try, she **nailed it**.

'I got it!' she said, pink from the effort. 'Um, want a quick skip? Since you helped?'

Are burgers the best food in the world? Do cranky cats called **ZEUS** drink from the toilet bowl?

'Sure,' I said, acting cool, even though I was **SO EXCITED** to skip some more!

So, Clover and I skipped. I did **double-crisscrosses** and Clover copied me, then we played Patty Cake as we skipped.

'Faster!' Clover called, and the ropes became a **BLUR**.

Faster and faster we skipped, our shoes hitting the ground in **perfect** time. We jumped out together and landed side by side.

Clover's face split into this wide, goofy smile, the one she stopped doing last year because she hated her braces. I smiled back.

'That was fun,' she said, panting.

And this is **weird**, but just for a moment, I remembered why I'd liked her.

THIS NEXT BIT IS SUPER EMBARRASSING, SO I'M WRITING IT SMALL AND MESSY SO ONLY I CAN READ IT . . .

SOMETIMES I MISS BEING FRIENDS WITH CLOVER WILLIAMS.

SOMETIMES I WISH WE COULD GO BACK TO HOW WE WERE, WHEN CLOVER WAS FIERCE AND FUNNY. WHEN WE DID ALL SORTS OF FUN THINGS TOGETHER, LIKE SOCCER AND ROCK CLIMBING, THINGS THAT MY OTHER FRIENDS DON'T ENJOY.

AND SOMETIMES I WISH CLOVER HADN'T RUINED EVERYTHING BY STEALING MY SQUISHY HAMBURGER KEYRING AND BECOMING MY MORTAL ENEMY!

BUT . . . IS CLOVER WILLIAMS STILL MY MORTAL ENEMY?

BECAUSE RIGHT NOW, I'M NOT SO SURE.

'Thanks for helping the **SHOOTING STARS**,' Clover said, tucking a strand of hair behind her ear.

I just nodded, super chill.

'See ya,' I said to her, and strolled back to the Friendship Tree.

'I'm all done with the Shooting Stars,' I said to my friends.

'They have a team name? **We need a team name!**' Grace said. She loves naming things. 'How about the Flying Fillies?'

UGH! Enough with those Filly Friends toys.

'Yes!' Otti said.

'OK, sure,' I said, since I didn't care about team names.

'I know—we could wear **costumes** to skip,' Otti said. 'We could be **UNICORNS!**'

'Yay, costumes!' Grace said, clapping her hands. 'I just saw this great video that shows you how to make unicorn horns out of headbands, modelling clay and **GLITTER!** Let's make those!'

Grace loves costumes even more than naming things. She says 'costumes' like most people say 'cake'—her eyes light up and she goes all **glowy**.

'I'm reading this series about a girl who owns a Pegasus,' Sienna said. 'What about a Pegasus costume?'

'Oh, I have fairy wings at home,' Otti said. 'I could be a Pegasus.'

'We could even be alicorns,' Grace said. 'They're even better than **PEGASUSES**. Alicorns have wings *and* a horn!'

Yep, my friends were more excited about the costumes than the skipping. Their costume ideas weren't exactly practical, either.

'Guys, how will we do **tricks and jumps** in fairy wings and unicorn horns?' I said, but no-one was listening.

'Is the mother of an alicorn a unicorn and the father a Pegasus?' Otti asked. 'Or do the parents of an alicorn both have to be alicorns?'

'Both are **ALICORNS**,' Sienna said.

'Are you sure?' Grace said.

'Absolutely,' Sienna replied.

Why were my friends talking about **MADE-UP ANIMALS** when we needed to practise?

'Otti, want to try the skier jumps?' I asked. 'Can you guys turn the ropes fast?'

But Grace and Sienna were too busy arguing about the parents of alicorns to turn the ropes properly. They kept stopping to **disagree**.

Across the playground, Clover was practising the squat-bounce. *Her* group turned the ropes perfectly all lunchtime.

Maybe I'm a bad friend, but I wish I could spend every lunchtime skipping with **CLOVER WILLIAMS!**

Grace

Friday, 3.52 p.m.,
at home

Last night, as I was doing my homework with Zeus at my feet, the front door opened. **Thumping** sounds came from the kitchen. Izzy and I looked at each other.

'What's going on?' Izzy asked.

I shrugged.

A few seconds later, Dad slipped into our bedroom and set a SHOPPING BAG on my desk.

'What is it?' I asked.

'Take a look, Gee,' Dad said.

I peered in and saw **dozens** of little purple packets. Dad had got me *heaps* of Filly Friends!

'Thank you, thank you, thank you!' I said, hugging him. 'This is the best week ever!'

'The guy at the check-out gave me **extras**, so you should have plenty,' Dad whispered. 'I also got the stable to put them in.'

Dad got me the Filly Friends *stable!* He's the **BEST DAD EVER!**

Just then, Mum called from the kitchen, 'Ivan, why did you buy **nineteen** packets of laundry powder?'

Izzy snorted. Dad put his finger to his lips to hush her.

'And twenty packets of rice?' Mum went on. 'Is the whole neighbourhood moving in? Are we storing food in case of an **EARTHQUAKE?'**

Izzy and I giggled.

'It was on **SPECIAL!**' Dad yelled.

'But where will we put it all?' Mum called back. 'Ivan?'

Dad raised his eyebrows.

'I'd better go,' he said, and slipped from the room. We could hear him in the kitchen, telling Mum he'd store the extra in the garage.

I tore open the packets, **squeaking** every time I got a new Filly Friend.

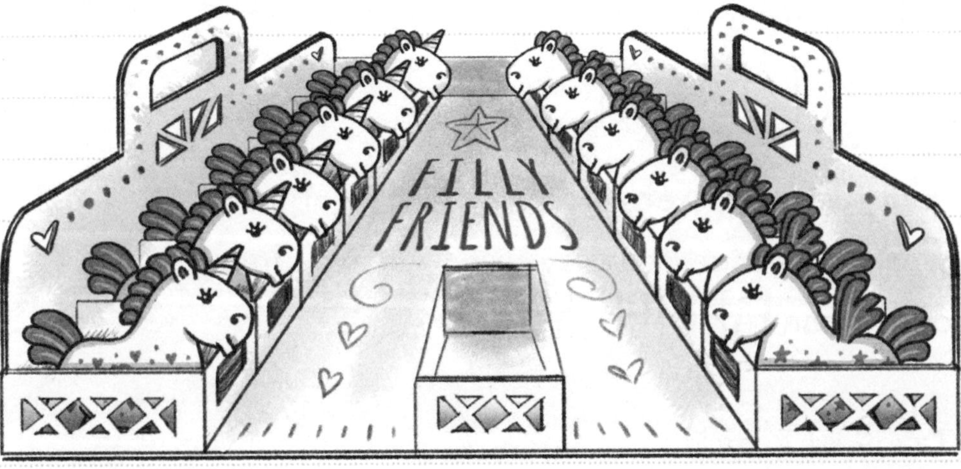

But when I opened the last packet and saw a purple unicorn, I felt a trickle of **disappointment**. I'd *hoped* for the Silver Alicorn.

Still, I had twelve out of the thirteen Fillies now, and a couple of doubles too, and the stable was **GORGEOUS!** I put my fillies in their stalls and arranged the doubles around my dolls.

I *really* wanted to put my **Sweet Sisters** dolls on the horses and take them for rides, but I couldn't in front of Izzy.

I fiddled with the white Pegasus, wishing she'd finish quickly and leave.

'Can I see that?' Izzy said, looking over.

I handed her the white Pegasus.

'**WHAT ARE YOU DOING!?**' I screeched, as the white Pegasus sailed through the air. It landed in the Mess Pile by her bed.

'Hey, I was just making it fly,' Izzy said.

Zeus padded over to sniff my Pegasus.

'No, no, no, no, no, no, no!' I said. I grabbed my precious Pegasus and gave Izzy a **sharp** look that meant, *Ziz, back off!*

'Relax,' she said. 'They're **plastic**. And what else are you supposed to do with them?'

'Collect them all,' I said firmly.

So, that was on Thursday. But you know how I told Dad it was the best week ever? Well, I was SILLY to say that on *Thursday* when there was still *Friday* to go.

Today, my soul is the colour of that ugly grey mansion up at Rocky Point. Mouldy Misery, that's how I feel. The skipping craze is stirring up so much trouble!

By the time Sienna and I reached the Friendship Tree at lunch today, the playground was **jammed**. Through the sea of kids, I spotted Izzy and Otti with Clover's group. Otti was talking to Izzy, who was eating something.

Sienna's eyes narrowed.

'What's Izzy doing?' she called, as Otti walked across the playground with our skipping ropes.

'Izzy's giving Clover's group skipping tips, 'cause Clem brought **RED VELVET CUPCAKES** to school and they're sharing with her,' Otti said, as she reached our tree.

'You're kidding,' Sienna said, looking at me.

One thing I *don't* like about being a twin is how people **expect** me to answer for Izzy.

'You know Izzy adores skipping and red velvet cake,' I said. 'I'm sure she'll be back in a minute. Let's start without her.'

Otti began our skipping routine, but after the karate kicks, she **stopped**, letting the ropes slap her ankles.

She seemed to be listening to a sound we couldn't hear.

'What?' Sienna said.

'My left arch,' Otti replied, stepping out of the ropes. She **flopped** under the Friendship Tree and wiggled off her shoe.

'Is it OK?' I asked.

'It's stiff,' Otti said. 'I can't risk it.'

Otti would be massaging her foot until the bell rang.

'I guess we're done with skipping for today,' I said, trying to sound **upset**.

Sienna stopped coiling the ropes.

'Grace,' she hissed. 'Look at Izzy.'

I followed Sienna's gaze. Izzy and Clover were skipping together in **PERFECT** time, grinning like they were having a **blast!**

'Are you *sure* Izzy's skipping with us for the TV crew?' Sienna asked.

A wave of hurt crashed over me. Sienna knows all about the **Great Squishy Hamburger Keyring Incident!** How can she think Izzy would dump us for Clover's group?

'I'm sure,' I said. 'Izzy loves the extra jumping time and cupcakes, but she *doesn't* love Clover Williams. Izzy's going to be a Flying Filly for the TV crew. Otti, tell her. You just spoke to Izzy. What did she say?'

Otti glanced up from her foot. 'When I asked Izzy when she was coming, she got a bit **annoyed** and said she'd be over soon,' Otti said. 'Then she started talking to Clover about the leapfrog trick. Maybe she just lost track of time?'

'She's over there with Clover instead of here with us,' Sienna said. 'What does that tell you?'

I felt sick. I couldn't believe **Sienna didn't trust Izzy!**

'It tells me Clover asked her to skip for a bit, that's all,' I said. 'You know Izzy always says yes to skipping. She even skips in her sleep.'

It's true. A few nights ago, I woke up to find Izzy counting out loud while she was fast asleep, her feet **pedalling** under the doona.

'You need to find out for sure, Grace,' Sienna said. 'Ask Izzy if she's still skipping with us.'

'Maybe you could ask her this weekend?' Otti said timidly. 'It can't hurt to check.'

That's another bad thing about being a twin—people ask me to talk to Izzy **for** them.

I should have said no. I should have told Sienna and Otti to ask Izzy themselves. But . . .

'OK,' I said.

So, I promised our friends I'd ask Izzy if she's going to be a Flying Filly or a Shooting Star.

Izzy's going to be SOOOOOO CRANKY. She's going to *hate* that our own friends doubted her!

Izzy

Saturday night

I'm writing this in the garage under Dad's old desk. Future Izzy T fans, I'm sure you want to know why I'm hiding out. Well, it's because I'm the **DIRTIEST RAT EVER!**

See, when I got home yesterday afternoon, I opened my bag and a packet of **super-sour** Fizz Missiles fell out.

Sticky-taped to the packet was a folded piece of paper. It read:

To Izzy,

Let's face it, you and I are the best skippers at RPP. In fact, we're awesome together—you know it's true.

So, will you please skip with the Shooting Stars next week? We'll blow everyone away! If you say yes, we'll add your leapfrog to our routine.

We're having a practice at Clem's house on Monday after school. Let me know Monday morning.

CLOVER

P.S. I forgot how much fun we have hanging out together. You're tons more fun than Clem and Harper, but don't tell them I said that.

WOW! I read the note over and over, especially the last bit. Was it true? We *did* have heaps of fun skipping together, and I was pretty sure she wasn't faking it.

Straightaway, I wanted to say **YES** to Clover. Problem was, I didn't know how to tell Grace. Keeping a secret from her makes me feel a hundred flavours of **BAD**, complete with **guilty** topping and **sneaky** sprinkles, so I'd been avoiding her.

After breakfast today, I headed to the concrete patch in the backyard. I wanted to learn this skipping move I'd seen online. It's called the **mic release** and can only be done by a single-rope skipper.

I propped Mum's tablet on top of the rubbish bin and followed the video instructions. I'd just got the hang of **swinging** the rope into a vertical arc next to my body, when the back door opened and Grace walked out with her toy stable. She lined up her Filly Friends on the steps, Zeus padding out to join her.

I felt all **HOLLOW**, like my insides had been scooped out with a sharp spoon. I'd have to tell her. I went back to my trick, but missed catching the handle. It snapped my ankle.

'Owww,' I said, rubbing it.

Grace picked up a pink Pegasus.

'Hey, Ziz,' she said slowly. 'Sienna and Otti want to know if you're skipping with us for the TV crew. I promised I'd check.'

She smiled at me in her **trusting** way, and I couldn't put it off any longer.

'Gee,' I said, letting her read my face.

If I'd told her I was giving up skipping to start the Rocky Point Chess Club, she couldn't have been more **SHOCKED**.

'Really? You're dumping us for *Clover's* group?' Grace asked.

I dipped my chin, *Yes.*

'Clover and I have been working on the leapfrog, the move that needs two people,' I said. 'We also want to do cartwheels. None of you guys can do those tricks with me.'

'So, Sienna was right,' Grace said, and I felt like the worst sister **EVER!**

'Sorry, Gee, but if Clover and I skip together, we'll be the **stars** of that video,' I said.

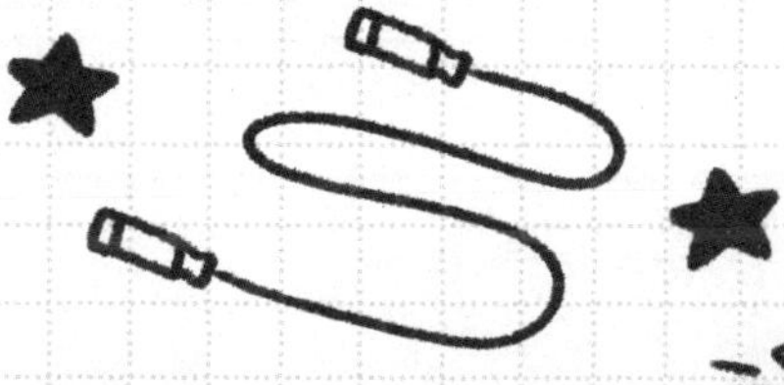

Looking at Grace was like looking into a mirror, except she looked like a sad cartoon kitten. She was **SO sad** I almost gave in and said I'd skip with the Flying Fillies.

But I don't want to skip with the Flying Fillies—I *want* to skip with the **SHOOTING STARS!**

'Mee noo, Ziz,' she said. That means 'I understand' in our twin language. 'If it was an art project, I'd want to be in the best group too.'

'Ah-moo, Gee,' I said, which means 'thank you'.

'But, Ziz, are you sure you won't get hurt?' Grace asked. 'After last time—'

'Hey, I'm **not** going to be friends with Clover again,' I said, butting in. 'This is **STRICTLY SKIPPING**.'

'OK, but you've got to tell Sienna and Otti yourself,' Grace said. 'I'm not being your messenger.'

I nodded. To tell you the truth, I'd been just about to ask Grace if she'd talk to Sienna and Otti for me. But I guess it will be OK. After all, telling them can't be as bad as telling Grace. She was so **disappointed** and worried about me!

The back door opened and Smelodie walked out with the washing basket, heading for the clothesline. For once, I was grateful the **Evil One** had arrived so we could stop talking about skipping teams.

As Smelodie stepped over Grace's toys, she said, 'Those big companies are sucking you in, Grace. I wouldn't have thought you'd fall for it at your age.'

Our big sister is **SO ANNOYING!** OK, I sort of agreed with her about the plastic horses. I don't know what Grace sees in them. She loves them more than the fake-fur cushion Baka, our grandma, got her for Christmas! And they don't do anything!

See, knowing Smelodie has taught me a lesson, and it's not about physics or whatever else she learns at her mega-brain school. No, the lesson is this: being clever is NOT the most important thing in life—it's more important **NOT TO BE A PAIN IN THE NECK!**

Grace and I **glared** at Smelodie.

'What?' she said, shrugging. 'It's the truth.'

The back door opened for the third time and Dad poked his head out. He was wearing his **scruffy** gym gear. Grace looked horrified—she cares about clothes.

'Mind if I join you?' he asked. 'I did a little skipping back at university when I boxed.' Dad swiped the air with some punches. 'Want to show me your stuff?'

I picked up the rope and showed Dad some **CRISSCROSSES** and **DOUBLE-UNDERS**.

'You're great, Iz,' Dad said. 'What tricks are you working on?'

'I'm learning a **mic release**,' I said, walking over to Mum's tablet and starting the video again. 'See?'

Dad squinted at the screen.

'Seems easy enough,' he said, holding out his hand for the rope.

The three of us girls shared a look.

'Dad, are you sure that's wise?' Smelodie asked.

I hated to agree with Smelodie **AGAIN**, but she had a point.

'Maybe you could go through it step by step with Izzy first?' Grace suggested.

'No, I've got it,' Dad said.

So, I passed him the rope and he started to **JUMP**.

Dad didn't *look* like he'd skipped much, but maybe he was rusty. After all, he went to university in the **super-olden** days when phones were still plugged into walls.

'Eighteen, nineteen, twenty!' Dad said, then let go of the handle like in the mic release video.

The handle leapt up and **WHACKED** him on the nose!

'OWWWWW!' Dad moaned, clutching his face. Blood dripped between his fingers and onto the concrete.

Grace shrieked and buried her face in her hands—she gets woozy when she sees **blood**.

'Dad!' I said, crouching beside him.

'What we should take from this,' Smelodie said to the empty air, 'is that old people shouldn't **judge** their fitness based on when they were young. Also, skipping is harder than it looks.'

Smelodie might be right again, but like Dad, her timing was **WAY OFF!**

'I'll get the icepack,' I said, jumping up.

Grace

Monday, 4.49 p.m.

I'm hiding under my doona in the depths of **despair!** *Anyone* would hide after what happened to me this afternoon.

I was leaving school with Otti when I realised I'd left my homework behind.

'I have to go back,' I said.

'See you tomorrow,' Otti replied, and **hurried off**. She seemed worried about her ballet exam on Friday.

I found my homework folder on my desk. As I crouched to slip it into my backpack, Ms Phillips, our librarian, paused near the doorway of the classroom.

'Look,' she said, lifting a white rubbish bag.

'More of those **FILLY HORSE** toys?' I heard Ms Kapoor call.

'The library's full of them after the kindergarten session,' Ms Phillips said. 'The kids even forget to open them!' She lifted the bag, which was slightly see-through. Inside, I saw **heaps** of purple packets.

Ms Phillips was talking about **unopened** *Filly Friends packets!*

I couldn't help myself. I zipped up my backpack and followed her onto the playground. She went around the office building to the big skip bins, so I **dawdled** behind a tree and watched.

Ms Phillips opened the skip bin with the blue lid and threw the bag in, slamming the lid shut. Sighing, she swept back around the building and disappeared.

I hurried to the skip bin and opened the lid.

YUCK! I thought, wrinkling my nose.

Even though the skip bin was only a quarter full, it stank. But that wasn't important, because I could see the rubbish bag. It had torn as it hit the bottom, and a purple packet showed through the split.

Now I *knew* there were unopened Filly Friends packets in that bag. What if the Silver Alicorn was in one of those packets, with its MELTY EYES and cute little hooves?

I had to save it!

I looked around. The playground was empty.

I grabbed the skip bin and **hoisted** myself up, wiggling so my hips were on the edge and leaning over so my head was inside.

Pheewww—it smelt terrible!

I reached for the bag. I was soooooo close, I could almost touch the handle!

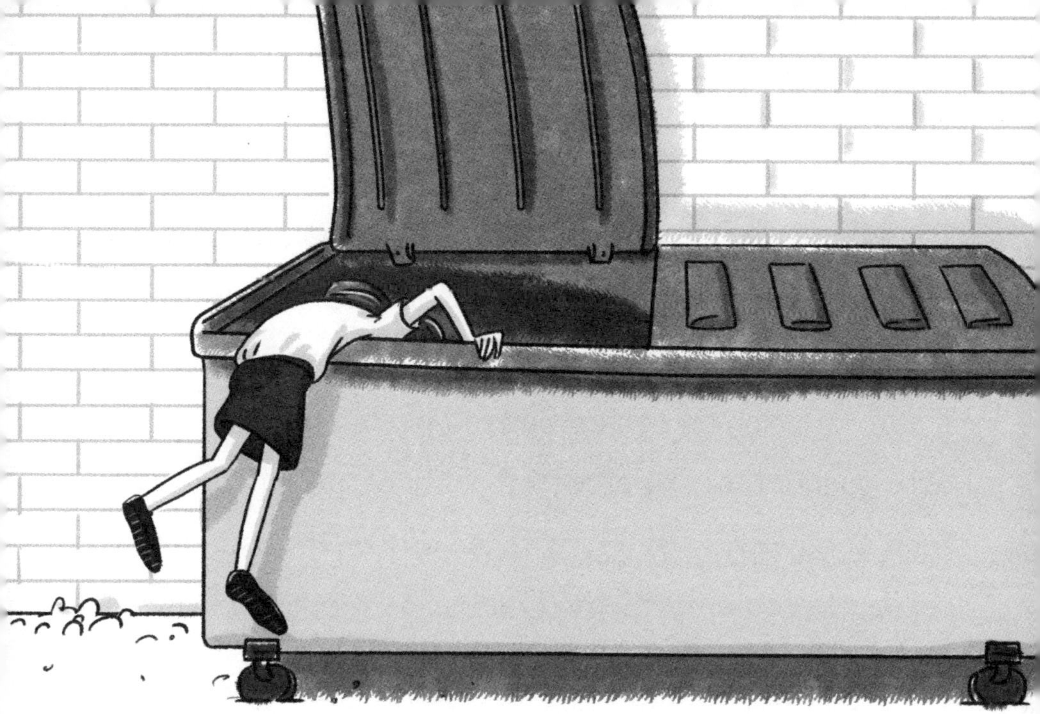

'Grace?' someone asked.

'Why have you got your head in a **DUMPSTER?!'** someone else said.

Clover Williams and Clem Chau!

I was so surprised, I lost my balance and slithered into the skip bin, **scraping** my elbow on the way down.

Oww!

I landed on my knees and gagged—I was surrounded by a **stench so strong**, I could almost see it. Even worse, the rubbish under my hands and knees was squishy! I was kneeling on rotten banana peels splattered with yoghurt, sticky slices of old ham, and a squishy tuna sandwich with a bite taken out of it. I suddenly remembered what Sienna had said—the kindy kids were tossing food in the recycling.

DISGUSTING!

My thoughts came in a flurry as I knelt there in the skip bin with the nastiest girls at school outside. Should I pretend I'd fallen in by accident? Should I pop up and say 'hi' as if it were no big deal, like I jumped into skip bins for fun? If I waited, would Clover and Clem just go away?

I didn't get a chance to say or do anything, because Clover and Clem's heads **appeared** over the rim of the skip bin.

'Gross, Grace!' Clover said, screwing up her nose.

'Did you jump in there to get those toys?' Clem asked.

'No,' I said.

'So, why are you holding that **rubbish** bag?' Clem said.

I looked at the bag in my hand and my face burned.

'No reason,' I said.

'I'm Grace Tomic and I **WUV** my horsey dollies,' Clem said in a baby voice.

Clover laughed.

'That's not very nice,' I said.

'That's not **vewwy** *nice!'* Clem said in the same baby voice.

My throat clogged up. Clover and Clem were **sooooo mean!**

'We'll leave you to it,' Clover said.

'See you later, **GARBAGE GIRL**,' Clem called, and their heads disappeared.

When they were gone, I tossed the rubbish bag of Filly Friends out of the skip bin and climbed out. I was sweaty and smelly and covered in garbage.

And guess what? I got sweaty and smelly and covered in garbage *for nothing!*

When I untied the rubbish bag, it was full of purple unicorns and **empty** Filly Friends packets. There were only three packets that weren't opened . . . and they were all purple unicorns.

I walked home, avoiding everyone I saw because I **stank**. I had a shower and put a bandaid on my elbow, but I might also need a long bath because I still smell like spoiled strawberry yoghurt.

I'm too **ashamed** to tell Izzy that I dived into a skip bin for Filly Friends.

I guess she's got other things to worry about, anyway. Izzy *still* hasn't told Sienna and Otti she's not jumping with the Flying Fillies, even though the TV crew's coming in two days. Whenever I bring it up, she says, 'I will, I promise.'

I wish she'd hurry up and tell them. It's kind of **UNFAIR**, because today I had to *lie* to Sienna and Otti and say I didn't know who Izzy was skipping with, when I really did. I could barely meet their eyes!

It's not like they haven't noticed that Izzy's hanging out so much with Clover and Clem! Everyone remembers how it ended with Clover last time Izzy was friends with her. I'm worried. Is it strictly skipping, like Izzy says, or **is she about to get hurt all over again?**

Izzy

Tuesday night, late

You know that big **mansion** at the top of Rocky Point, the one that looks like a grey box that Grace hates? Well, guess who lies in that mansion's pool on her blow-up flamingo, staring at her phone?

CLEM CHAU, that's who. And Clover and Harper when they visit, probably.

Clem's house is *amazing!* It has five bedrooms and six bathrooms, and get this . . . only four people live there! How come we have to share two bathrooms between our whole family and Clem's family get **ONE-AND-A-BIT BATHROOMS EACH?!** Oh, and the floor is this shiny, polished concrete that I'd LOVE to skateboard on! Although, I think there's a no-skateboarding-inside-the-mansion rule, because Clem's mum hurried me into the garden when I pulled Smelodie's skateboard out of my bag.

When I got there yesterday, a delivery driver arrived with tons of shopping. He also brought in five bulging bags of those horse toys that Grace loves. Clem says her little sister's crazy for them.

Clem and Clover also designed our skipping costumes, and Clem's mum actually had them **MADE!** Who does that? They're purple tank tops with shooting stars in silver sequins on them. **PUKE!** But since I want to skip with the Shooting Stars, I'll shut up and wear the sequins.

Anyway, tonight we filmed our skipping routine on Clem's phone and watched it on her big TV. It's looking **awesome**.

What's not so awesome is what happened at recess today between me and Sienna. When Grace and I arrived at the Friendship Tree, we found Sienna and Otti waiting with the skipping ropes.

'Filly here, ready to fly,' Sienna said.

Grace shot me this **pleading look**. *Gon, Ziz,* she was saying. That means 'Come on!' or 'Hurry up!' in our twin language.

Cornered or what? I *had* to tell Sienna and Otti then and there.

'I'm really sorry, but I'm not skipping with you guys for the TV crew,' I said in a rush. Talk about awkward.

'You're only telling us this now?' Sienna said, putting her hands on her hips. 'The day before the TV crew comes?'

I felt **TERRIBLE!**

'Sorry,' I mumbled again.

Sienna **raised** her eyebrows.

'So, Otti's going to do the routine alone while Grace and I turn the ropes?' she said. 'And since Otti can't do the cartwheel and splits before her exam, it won't be very exciting, will it?'

'Sienna, I think she gets it,' Otti muttered.

'Oh, I'm not sure she does,' Sienna said, jabbing her finger at me. 'I'm not sure she knows how **selfish** she's being. And all because she's desperate to be a skipping star!'

WAIT A SECOND! Sienna was calling me selfish? The reason the Flying Fillies were boring without me was because none of *them* took skipping seriously. I came up with the whole routine! I learned the tricks! I was the only one who bothered to practise!

There's this thing that happens to me when I get angry. The anger **builds** inside me until I feel like a superhero with hot lasers that burst out of my eyes. Well, my anger was building and Sienna was about to be zapped into **BURNT TOAST!**

'You're not a teacher, Sienna, so stop acting like one,' I snapped. Grace put her hand on my shoulder, but I shrugged her off. 'I just want to skip with people who care about skipping. At least the Shooting Stars practise!'

Sienna went **BRIGHT RED**.

'It's not about practice!' Sienna yelled. 'It's about loyalty to your friends!'

'Sienna . . .' Otti said, but Sienna gave her the **bug-eyed** glare and Otti shut her mouth.

'Of course it's about practice,' I yelled back. 'And how were you loyal to me? You didn't even bother to learn double-dutch, and now you're trying to make me feel bad? If you want a good routine, Sienna, **LEARN SOME TRICKS YOURSELF!**'

We glared at each other. Sienna's so rigid, she makes a **METAL RULER** look relaxed!

Grace

Tuesday, 8.13 p.m.

DRAMA, DRAMA, DRAMA! Today had more drama in it than the day Izzy accidentally let a huntsman spider loose in the library. Soraya Savvas was screaming at the top of her lungs by the time Ms Phillips caught it in a mug and put it outside.

Every time Clover and Clem and Harper passed me today, they whispered 'Garbage girl!' and wrinkled their noses like I **stank**.

That was bad, but the drama *really* got out of control at recess when Izzy told Sienna and Otti that she was skipping with the Shooting Stars. Izzy and Sienna had a **massive** fight. They yelled so loudly that everyone stared! I was wondering how to calm them down, when Sienna turned to me.

'Grace, tell her how selfish she's being,' she said.

What?

Both Sienna and Izzy were glaring at *me*. Their eyes felt like **MAGNIFYING GLASSES** with the sun blasting through them.

'Well . . .' I said.

On the one hand, Sienna was right. Izzy should have told the team earlier. On the other hand, if someone had talent, shouldn't they be **ALLOWED TO SHINE?**

'. . . it's tricky,' I finished.

Neither of them liked that answer. Izzy rolled her eyes.

Sienna said, 'Of course you think that because she's your twin.'

That **stung**.

'That's not fair,' Otti said, and I shot her a grateful look. 'I bet Grace really thinks that.'

'I do,' I said.

'Well, I think it's **rotten** and I never want to talk to you again, Izzy Tomic!' Sienna said, throwing the skipping ropes to the ground and **MARCHING OFF** towards the library. She cut right across the Year 4 kids' handball game, ignoring the yells.

Otti watched Sienna go.

'I'd better check she's OK,' she said, and hurried after Sienna.

Izzy and I were left alone under the Friendship Tree.

'Oh nooooo!' Izzy said.

I gave a tiny shake of my head, meaning, *You can't blame her.*

Izzy's shoulders **sagged**.

'You're right,' she said. 'I should have said something before.'

We shared a look. *Bad, bad, bad!* we were both saying.

A flash of lime-green caught my eye. Over on the basketball courts, Clem and Harper were **shaking out** the best skipping ropes, while Clover fixed her hair.

'The Shooting Stars are waiting for you,' I said.

Izzy gave me a gentle punch on the arm.

'Thanks,' she said.

I shrugged, which meant, *No worries,* and she hurried off.

Later, at lunchtime, the playground echoed with the **snap, snap, snap** of turning ropes.

When Otti and I arrived at the Friendship Tree, Sienna handed us a crisp sheet of paper.

'Our new routine,' she said proudly.

SIENNA BURNS' FAIR & FUN SKIPPING ROUTINE

(ONLY SKIPPED WITH ONE ROPE BECAUSE SIENNA AND GRACE CAN'T JUMP DOUBLE-DUTCH.)

OTTI SKIPS SIDE-TO-SIDE SKIER BOUNCES, FIFTY SECONDS

SWITCH ROPES, FIVE SECONDS

GRACE SKIPS SIDE-TO-SIDE SKIER BOUNCES, FIFTY SECONDS

SWITCH ROPES, FIVE SECONDS

SIENNA SKIPS SIDE-TO-SIDE SKIER BOUNCES, FIFTY SECONDS

FINISH!

Sienna patted the **STOPWATCH** around her neck.

'I'll make sure everyone gets equal time,' she said.

Otti and I shared a look as Sienna picked up the skipping rope and passed me a handle.

'One, two, three, go!' Sienna said, clicking the stopwatch.

Otti skipped obediently.

'And . . . **switch!**' Sienna called after fifty seconds, and Otti jumped out of the rope and took my handle.

I jumped into the rope.

'Switch!' Sienna called after **fifty** seconds, and I jumped out and took Sienna's handle.

'Switch!'

'This is a bit boring,' Otti whispered, as she took my rope handle.

I nodded. Not only was our routine dull without tricks, but each time we switched, everything **stopped**.

'Switch!' Sienna called again.

'What about Otti does the karate kicks?' I suggested.

'That wouldn't be fair because you and I can't do karate kicks,' Sienna pointed out.

As I turned the rope, I watched the Shooting Stars from the corner of my eye.

'Wow,' Otti said, letting the rope **SMACK** her legs. 'The Shooting Stars are awesome!'

'We're good too,' Sienna said, glaring at the Shooting Stars. 'Sure, they've got **FLASHY TRICKS**, but *we're* skipping like a real team. Come on, Otti, switch! Switch!'

The mood was the same after school at Otti's house.

'When we finish these, we'll practise our switches again,' Sienna said, as we plaited purple-and-white strips of fabric into tails. '**PRACTICE MAKES PERFECT**, after all.'

Otti looked at me in horror. We'd already spent hours on the switches.

'I think we've nailed the switches, Sienna,' I said.

Just then, Otti's mum called from the hall.

'What pizzas do you want, girls?'

We looked at the **empty spot** on Otti's rug where Izzy usually sat.

'We won't be needing the Meat Lover's with extra bacon today,' Sienna said.

'Just a Margarita and a Hawaiian, thanks, Mum,' Otti called back.

Sienna **jumped** up and put on a unicorn headband. She posed in front of Otti's mirror.

'Our costumes look great,' she said. 'We don't need Izzy.'

Down on the rug, Otti and I shared a **SAD LOOK**.

And now, I'm waiting for Izzy to get home. She's still at Clem's house skipping with the Shooting Stars.

The sun set a long time ago, but a tiny sliver of moon is rising. I can make out Zeus's **BIG EYES** in the darkness. Even though she's a cat, she knows how much I hate all this **drama**.

I really don't care who Izzy skips with!

ALL I **CARE** ABOUT IS:

1. Finding the Silver Alicorn.
2. That Clover never tells Izzy I went dumpster-diving!
3. And most important of all, that our group are friends again.

Izzy

Wednesday, after school

This morning, as I walked to school with Grace, I kept thinking about the **HUGE FIGHT** I'd had with Sienna yesterday. I felt angry, then guilty, then angry all over again. Sienna's **IMPOSSIBLE!**

Grace and I reached the school gate and turned to each other.

'Gooloo, Ziz.'

'Gooloo, Gee.' That means 'good luck' in our twin language.

Shoulder to shoulder, we walked inside. And then we stopped and stared. Rocky Point Primary looked like a **super-fancy** school on Open Day! The playground was litter-free, the windows **SPARKLED**, the veggie garden was weeded, everyone's school shoes were shiny and their hair was tightly plaited with ribbons.

I touched my own messy hair. Oh well.

As we walked past the Friendship Tree where Sienna and Otti were sitting, I paused.

'Good luck, guys,' I said. I'm not a **MONSTER**. Although we're not skipping together, I still wanted the Flying Fillies to do well.

'Good luck, Izzy,' Otti said. 'You'll be great.'

At least Otti doesn't hate me. I turned to Sienna, who was **STARING UP** into the tree.

'Sienna?'

'I don't talk to **TRAITORS**,' she said to the leaves.

I got a sick feeling then, the same one I get when our school reports come out.

Otti's face fell. Grace tilted her head, meaning *Give her some time*.

On my way to class, I spotted Crome Dome. He was playing with his tie as he spoke to a woman with curly dark hair and a guy with a video camera. **The TV crew had arrived!**

Crome Dome had given us a few rules. We weren't allowed to skip until lunchtime, because the camera crew wanted shots of kids running around at recess. Also, if the crew came into our classrooms, we were supposed to act like they weren't there.

The camera crew **DID** visit our class during science. It was tricky because Mr Rafael was talking about the types of rocks on the planet Mercury—so **BORING!**—but I put on my listening face and nodded like a car-dashboard toy.

Then the bell finally rang! It was time for the Shooting Stars to **blast** out of the solar system!

Clem led us through the office towards the **teachers' toilet** and opened it with Mrs Allsop's big set of keys.

'Mrs Allsop said the Shooting Stars are allowed to use the teachers' toilet to get changed,' Clem said. 'But only us.'

I got changed in one of the toilet stalls. FYI, the teachers' toilet is a **TOTAL LETDOWN**. It's just a boring bathroom with grey tiles. Grace is going to be **SUPER** disappointed!

When I came out, Clover was brushing her hair and our eyes met in the mirror. She looked **nervous**.

'Hey, you're going to be great,' I said, smiling at her. 'We just have to **ignore the camera**.'

'Totally,' Clover said, forcing a smile. 'Shooting Stars forever.' She crouched to put away her brush. When she stood up, she seemed calm again.

As a team, we walked onto the playground, where kids and teachers were gathering on the basketball courts. We were almost there when Clover stopped.

'Uh-oh,' she said, lifting her bare wrist. 'I think I **DROPPED MY BRACELET** in the teachers' toilet. Izzy, do you mind going back and getting it for me?'

'Sure,' I said. 'I just need the key.'

'I'm the only one allowed to use the keys,' Clem huffed. As she spoke, loud music **blared** across the playground.

We looked at each other. The skipping was about to start!

'How about you open the toilet for Izzy, then run back to open the shed for the skipping ropes?' Clover suggested.

'OK,' Clem agreed, and Clem and I **hurried off**.

The office was **DESERTED**. Clem unlocked the teachers' toilet again and we peered around.

'What does Clover's bracelet look like?' I asked.

'It's silver,' Clem said from the doorway. 'Maybe she dropped it while she was doing her hair?'

Then, as I crouched to look under the sink, the door **SLAMMED** behind me and the lock **CLICKED!**

'See you after lunch, loser!' Clem called through the door.

In one crushing moment, I understood. Clem Chau had **LOCKED ME INSIDE THE TEACHERS' TOILET!**

I sprang up and grabbed the handle, but the door was definitely locked. I was so angry, I nearly cried, and I **NEVER** cry. I slid to the floor.

With me trapped in the teachers' toilet, I wouldn't be in the video at all. The Shooting Stars would star Clover Williams **SOLO!**

Was it all a set-up? Were the red velvet cupcakes, the Fizz Missiles, the note and the practice sessions at school and Clem's house all planned to suck me in and trick me? Or had Clover cut me out at the last minute?

I don't know for sure, and I probably never will. And even though I'm mad at myself for trusting her, most of all it **hurts**.

I TRULY THOUGHT CLOVER WILLIAMS AND I COULD BE FRIENDS, OR AT LEAST SKIPPING BUDDIES.

As the pop music floated through the little window above the sink, I wanted to scream. I'd been played by **CLOVER WILLIAMS—AGAIN!**

Grace

Wednesday, 4.45 p.m.

When the bell rang for lunch, the students who weren't skipping ran to grab their spots beside the basketball courts, ready to cheer us on. The skipping teams got changed and waited by the fence. Pop music was blasting through the speakers—Mrs Allsop had turned it up **loud!**

Sienna slung our rope around her shoulders like a scarf.

'Hold onto your horns because the Flying Fillies are going to blow everyone away!' she said.

Otti adjusted her **UNICORN-HORN HEADBAND**, which had slipped over her eyes.

I rubbed my sweaty hands on my top. I wasn't a great skipper—what if I tripped on camera? What if I missed one of the switches? What if my unicorn tail slid down like undies that had lost their elastic?

Near us, the Shooting Stars looked cool and **unfussed**. Clem and Harper shook out the lime-green ropes, while Clover smoothed her hair. I had to admit, their costumes were ADORABLE. Clem even had a silver bag to match the shooting star on her top. But . . .

'Where's Izzy?' I wondered.

Sienna raised an eyebrow.

'Who cares?' she said.

'Don't be like that,' Otti said, tugging up the waistband of her tail.

The skipping was about to start, but the Shooting Stars didn't seem bothered that **IZZY WAS MISSING**. Something didn't feel right.

'Back in a sec,' I said.

I circled the crowd, heading for the girls' toilets. Maybe Izzy was there, which would explain why the Shooting Stars were so calm.

But the toilets were **empty**.

I checked the classroom, then trekked past the Friendship Tree. At the sand pit, I stopped and gazed towards the basketball courts. The TV producer and cameraman were deep in discussion. I needed to head back, but a weird, **nagging** feeling told me to keep going. I turned towards the office.

As soon as I stepped inside the corridor, I heard a **thud, thud, thud** coming from the teachers' toilet.

'Ziz?' I said.

'Gee!' Izzy called, her voice **muffled**. She was inside the teachers' toilet and she was furious!

'They've locked me in! I never should have trusted Clover Williams!' Izzy yelled. 'She wants me to miss the filming so she can be the SOLO STAR.'

'Hang on,' I said.

I jiggled the handle, but the door was **locked**.

'Let me try outside!' I ran back outside and behind the building, **wincing** at the skip bin with the blue lid next to the wall there, and gazed up at the little window that led to the teachers' toilet.

'You need to stop the filming, get the key and **let me out** of here,' Izzy called from the open window. 'Everyone needs to know what filthy cheats they are!'

'But won't that cause a fuss in front of the TV crew?' I said. 'RPP will look bad and Mr Crome won't be pleased.'

'Yeah, you're right,' Izzy groaned.

'So, what do we do?' I asked.

We thought about it.

'How about I **climb out** of the window?' Izzy said. 'I reckon I can reach it if I get up on the sink.'

'Can you fit through?' I asked. The window looked **AWFULLY** small.

'I think so,' Izzy said. 'But it might take some squirming

time. While I do that, you can join the Shooting Stars and pretend to be me!'

'Uh, excuse me?' I said. I **COULDN'T SKIP** like Izzy! 'Maybe I could get up on the bin and help you climb out instead?'

'That won't save time,' Izzy said. 'Do anything you can to **stop** the Shooting Stars from skipping without me!'

Izzy's balled-up Shooting Stars top came flying out of the window and landed on my dumpster.

'Leave your Flying Fillies costume out there for me,' Izzy called.

I wavered.

'You don't have to skip, just stop them from starting,' Izzy said. 'Come on, it's **ZIZANGEE TIME!**'

Izzy's my twin and my **BFFFF** (that means 'triple forever'). What else could I do?

I ripped off my unicorn costume, slipped on the Shooting Stars' top and **messed up** my hair to look like Izzy's.

Then I took a deep breath. It whooshed out all shaky. *Steady*, I told myself, *Izzy needs you.*

'Just for the record,' I called. 'Are there really **GOLD TAPS** and rose-scented soap in the teachers' toilet?'

'I'll tell you later,' Izzy snorted. 'Now go!'

I hurried back to the playground. The teams were spread across the basketball courts, ready to begin. Everyone **turned** as I approached.

'Isabel Tomic, where have you been?' Mr Crome called.

'Bathroom, Mr C,' I called back in **IZZY-MODE**.

After years of practice, I'm great at being Izzy. Although, I don't usually pretend to be my twin in front of a film crew.

As I **swaggered** towards the Shooting Stars, Clover made a sound like Zeus coughing up a **HAIRBALL**. Clem and Harper stared.

'How . . .' Clem said.

Then Sienna and Otti saw me. Sienna turned away, but Otti hurried over.

'Izzy!' she said. 'Do you know where Grace went? She's **DISAPPEARED!**'

Even *Otti* believed I was Izzy! I wanted to tell her the truth, but couldn't risk it.

'Nope, sorry,' I said. I only hoped Izzy would arrive quickly so the Flying Fillies got a chance to skip.

Mr Crome waved his arms for **attention**.

'RPP, let's do this!' he called over the music. 'Skippers, begin!'

The producer nodded at the cameraman. A tiny red light appeared on his camera.

Across the basketball courts, ropes began to turn.

Clover stood on the other side of the lime-green ropes that were going **smack, smack, smack, smack, smack, smack**. She glared at me and then she glared at the ropes.

Suddenly, I realised Clover was about to start, and I was supposed to jump in with her!

I knew I couldn't skip **DOUBLE-DUTCH** without face-planting and breaking my nose. I *had* to stop the filming!

'Whoa, whoa, whoa!' I hollered, running straight at the cameraman. I stood in front of the camera and did stretches. 'Got to get warm.'

The red light on the camera **winked** off. The cameraman popped up, looking puzzled.

'Kid, you can't stand there,' he explained. 'You're **RUINING** my shot.'

The other ropes stopped turning. As the Rocky Point students giggled and whispered, I did some jumping jacks. It was **SOOOOOO EMBARRASSING** that I'm burning up again as I write this! Izzy owes me.

Mr Crome sidled over, his left eyelid twitching.

'Isabel Tomic, what are you doing?' he hissed. 'The *Minister for Education* is going to see this video!'

I wanted to **throw** myself at his feet and scream, 'I'm not Izzy, Mr Crome! *I'm Grace!*' Instead, I grinned and said, 'Don't want to sprain an ankle, Mr C.'

The TV producer signalled to Mr Crome and he raced over to speak to her. After a minute, he waved at the Shooting Stars.

'There's been a **change** of plan,' he called. 'Isabel Tomic and the Shooting Stars, wait by the fence. Everyone else, you can now begin your routines again.'

The Shooting Stars stalked to the fence. Clover was sending me evil looks, but I ignored her. I kept glancing towards the office. Where was Izzy? Was she **STUCK** halfway out of the window?

Then, Clover whispered something to Clem and Clem **sidled** along the fence towards me.

'It's over, garbage girl,' she hissed. 'You've got that graze on your arm from falling into the dumpster. Let us skip, or we'll tell Mr Crome you're not Izzy.'

I touched the **bandaid** on my elbow, then closed my eyes. I was caught. Still, I couldn't let Clover sabotage my sister.

'Go for it,' I said, opening my eyes. 'And I'll tell Mr Crome you locked Izzy in the teachers' toilet.'

Clover's mouth was a hard, tight line. She nodded at Clem.

'We've got an offer for you,' Clem said. 'We know how much you **LOVE** those Filly Friend dollies. Hey, you love them so much you dived into the rubbish for them. So, if you stop pretending to be Izzy *right now*, I'll give you . . .'

Clem put her hand into her bag and felt around. Slowly, she drew something out.

There, on Clem's palm, was a **Silver Alicorn!** It was so perfect, it seemed to glow from the inside!

Noooooooooooo!

Izzy

Wednesday night, in the garage

It took me a while to climb out of the teachers' toilet, because the window was higher than I'd thought. Luckily, I'm an **awesome** rock climber. Only thing is, my sneakers left dirty marks all over the sink and wall. I hope Crome Dome never figures out who made the mess!

As I ran across the playground in Grace's unicorn outfit, the producer spotted me. Her eyes widened.

'**TWINS!**' she shouted. She had the thrilled look that people sometimes get when they see Grace and I together. '**IDENTICAL TWINS! FILM THEM!**'

For a few seconds, I thought we'd need an ambulance, because Crome Dome looked like he was having a heart attack.

'Grace? Isabel?' he **hissed**. 'I don't care who you are, just get out there and skip!'

As I ran towards her, Grace sagged with relief. She stuck out her hand and we **FIST-BUMPED**. The other teams were almost finished when the Shooting Stars ran onto the basketball court.

As Clem and Harper turned the ropes, I took my place and gave Clover my best **DEATH GLARE**. She glared back.

'You're not even wearing the right costume,' Clover hissed.

'As if I care!' I hissed back, **tossing** the wings, unicorn headband and tail aside. Like I said, not practical for skipping.

When the camera turned to us, Clover and I stuck on these **fake** grins. Together, we jumped into the ropes for the Shooting Stars' routine.

'You're a **DIRTY** cheat, Williams,' I muttered as we skipped.

'And you're a sad loser, Tomic,' she said, smiling her brains out as we **HEEL-TAPPED**.

As I leapfrogged over Clover, I said to the back of her head, 'What kind of coward locks someone in a toilet because they're **jealous?**'

One by one, the other teams finished their routines and watched us. Clover jumped out and it was time for my solo. As I skipped, all of Rocky Point Primary clapped in time to the music—the kids, the teachers, even the producer. It felt **AMAZING!**

But then Grace met my eyes. She tipped her head and pointed her finger at Clem. Even from that distance, I could read her.

She was telling me **CLEM WAS ABOUT TO TRIP ME UP ON CAMERA!**

I was so shocked I almost tripped myself up. Clover nodded, and Clem stared at my feet. She was about to **yank** the handles. There was no way to stop her . . .

All at once, Sienna yelled, '**SWITCH!**'

Sienna and Grace ran over. Smoothly, they grabbed the skipping-rope handles from Clem and Harper and shoved them aside.

For a moment, the ropes stopped and everything was a **mess**. Then Sienna and Grace started turning and I caught the beat.

Clem and Harper gaped like **stunned** goldfish. Clover was drooling with rage!

'Filly time!' Grace called.

Otti ran over, jumped in and started doing skier bounces.

I smiled **CRAZILY** at her, getting it. We were going to do the ITFSR together, but this time it was The Flying Fillies' Fierce Skipping Routine (TFFFSR)!

Sienna and Grace turned fast, and Otti forgot about her ballet exam and skipped at **SUPER** speed. Otti's an awesome skipper when she tries.

I finished our routine by cartwheeling out and landing the splits. When I looked over, I saw Otti beside me. She'd done the cartwheel and splits too.

YESSSS!

As everyone but the Shooting Stars clapped, I caught Clover's eye. I couldn't believe she'd sabotaged me **again**, especially when we'd had so much fun.

'Really?' I mouthed at her, and something weird happened. Clover's face sort of crumpled, like she was about to cry. For a second, she looked . . . **GUILTY?** Or sad, maybe? Then she wouldn't look at me again.

Maybe some friendships can **never** work, even if the person you wanted to be friends with is fierce and funny and a terrific skipper. That stuff's not enough if you can't trust them.

So, Clover and I are back to being **MORTAL ENEMIES!**

Wait, I can hear Dad calling us for dinner.

OK, I'm back.

FYI, I **HATE** saying sorry. I'd rather do thirty-five pages of maths homework than say sorry. I'd rather eat a chunky slug from our garden than say sorry. Still, I knew it was the right thing to do.

After the last bell today, Grace and I waited under the Friendship Tree until Sienna and Otti came by. Otti stopped, but Sienna was about to stalk right past when I called out to her.

'Guys, I'm sorry I **dumped** you like that for the Shooting Stars. I should have told you how I was feeling earlier. And, Sienna, thanks for saving me when Clem was about to **trip** me up.'

Sienna stared at the ground for ages.

'I'm sorry I yelled,' she finally said. 'That wasn't fair, because we've never been as **SERIOUS** as you about skipping. I knew that bothered you and I get why you wanted to skip with Clover's group. The whole situation was—'

'—tricky?' Grace finished, with a tiny smile.

'Yes,' Sienna said. 'Sometimes things aren't as simple as **right and wrong**.'

Grace, Otti and I gaped. Sienna had never said anything like that before!

'But mostly, they are that simple,' she added.

We **BURST OUT** laughing.

'What?' she said, offended. 'It's true.'

Sienna might be crazy about fairness and rules, but I also trust her and she's **SUPER** loyal.

And hey, no-one's perfect. Not even me. I mean, I'm 99.99999% perfect, but there's still 0.0001% that isn't. (And I don't care if my maths is wrong.)

As our laughter died away, Grace **elbowed** me.

She'd said an apology had two parts. First, I had to say sorry and **mean** it. Second, I had to try to **FIX** the damage.

'I promise I'll turn the ropes every break so you guys get a skip, to make up for it,' I said.

Sienna shook her head.

'Izzy, I don't want to skip anymore.'

'Me either,' Otti said.

I turned to Otti in **surprise**.

'But, Otti, you're amazing,' I said. 'You could be the best skipper on the playground if you tried.'

'I miss eating lunch,' Otti said, shrugging.

I turned back to Sienna.

'I could teach you double-dutch—' I started, but Sienna shook her head.

'No, thanks,' she said. 'I'm **sick** of skipping.'

'What about you?' I asked Grace.

'I hate skipping!' Grace **burst out**.

I stared at her.

'You *hate* skipping?' I said.

Grace nodded. Her face was **BRIGHT PINK**.

'Yes,' she said in a small voice. 'I didn't want to tell you.'

I was shocked. If anyone in the world knows how Grace is feeling, it's me. How did I miss something so big?!

'So, **ALL** of you want to stop skipping?' I said.

They nodded.

'OK, I get it,' I said.

I guess I'll have to skip with someone else from now on. Willow's a good skipper and I know her from soccer—she's super nice. Maybe she'll let me skip with her group? I'll ask her tomorrow.

'If you don't want to skip, how can I make it up to you?' I asked Sienna and Otti.

Straightaway, Sienna said, 'You can help me sort out the kindy bins this week.'

So, because I'm a **kind** and **decent** friend who says sorry, I'm spending the rest of the week fishing smelly banana peels out of the **RECYCLING** bins!

PUKE!

Grace
Friday, 4.29 p.m., on the balcony

It's been **three weeks** since the TV crew came to Rocky Point Primary, and today, we watched the video on our classroom screens.

RPP was one of three schools featured, and we got lots more time than the other two! The final minutes of the video showed the skipping.

First, we saw all the groups skipping, then it cut to me 'stretching'. Next, Izzy ran over and we fist-bumped. Then Izzy and Clover skipped together in **PERFECT** time, with the camera on Izzy so you could only see the back of Clover's head. Then the video cut to me and Sienna 'switching' smoothly. (Sienna's switching practice really paid off!) It ended with Izzy and Otti doing perfect cartwheels and splits.

I was so **proud** of us all.

Later, as I walked across the playground, I passed the Shooting Stars huddled over Clover's phone.

'You're right there, see?' Clem was saying to Clover, whose eyes were **RED** and **swollen**. 'That's definitely the back of your head behind Izzy's arm.'

I couldn't help feeling a bit **SORRY** for Clover. She takes these things sooooo seriously.

After school, as Izzy, Otti, Sienna and I were walking out, the Year 1 girl who'd given me my first Filly Friend came over and **tugged** at Izzy's arm.

'Someone said Clem Chau gave you a Silver Alicorn,' she said, gazing up at Izzy.

'It was me, and I didn't take it,' I said, stepping forwards.

'Why not?' the girl asked.

I love little kids and can't wait to be in the **BUDDY PROGRAM** later this year, so I took the chance to teach a younger kid about friendship.

'Clem wanted me to **betray** my sister for the Silver Alicorn,' I said. 'I couldn't do that. Being loyal is more important than any Filly Friend.'

The girl went slack-jawed.

'That's so **dumb**,' she said. 'She's stuck being your sister, so who cares if you betray her? She'd get over it and you'd have the Silver Alicorn.'

Izzy snorted with laughter.

'She's kind of right,' Izzy said.

'It will make sense when you're **older**,' I told the girl, but she just walked off, shaking her head.

Sienna and Otti were laughing too. In fact, my friends thought it was **HILARIOUS!**

Well, I wasn't laughing. Honestly, I was shocked! What's happened to little kids these days?

Grace

Friday, 8.45 p.m.,
before bed

It's way past bedtime, but I had to write this down! The most **AMAZING** thing just happened!

After dinner, I'd set up my Filly Friends' stable on the rug. Zeus sat beside me, **purring**.

I touched the floor of the one empty stall. If I closed my eyes, I could see the Silver Alicorn in Clem's hand. It **glowed**! I was thinking that maybe that Year 1 girl was right and I should have just taken the alicorn.

Then the bedroom door opened and Izzy appeared. She flopped on her bed.

'What are you up to?' she asked.

I gave a tiny shrug, which means **nothing**.

Then Izzy saw the stable.

'Oh yeah!' she said, rolling off her bed. She reached into her school backpack and pulled out three purple packets.

A little **FLUTTER** started in my throat.

'I found these cleaning out the kindy bins and forgot about them,' Izzy said. 'Ah-moo, Gee.' That means 'thank you' in our twin language.

'Ah-moo for what?' I said.

'For covering for me in the skipping,' she said. 'That couldn't have been easy.' Then she pulled a face that meant, *I know you hate* **everyone staring** *at you.*

I shrugged back. *You're my sister*, that meant. *I'd do anything for you.*

Izzy tossed the purple packets to me.

'Three more chances, Gee,' she said, and joined me on the rug.

I ripped the first open. A **PURPLE UNICORN** fell out.

As I ripped the second, Izzy scooted closer . . . it was another purple unicorn.

We burst out laughing, **breaking** the tension.

I picked up the third packet. Even though I knew it was unlikely, a teeny part of me still *hoped*.

I started to tear and saw . . . a **FLASH** of silver.

'No way!'
Izzy yelled,
punching
the air.
'No way!'

Into my hand
fell a Silver
Alicorn.

'You got it!' Izzy yelled. 'I got it for you!'

So, that's my big news! **I have the Silver Alicorn** and it's *gorgeous*!

Gently, I set it in its stall and admired my stable. My Filly Friends collection was **COMPLETE**.

'Ah–moo, Ziz,' I whispered.

'Hey, I've just worked out what you're supposed to do with them,' Izzy said. She slid off the bed.

I **narrowed** my eyes at her, meaning *Don't throw my Filly Friends into your Mess Pile again.*

Izzy lay on her stomach, picked up the purple unicorn and white Pegasus, and made them **trot** across the rug.

'Hi, I'm a unicorn,' she said in a **SQUEAKY** voice, wiggling the unicorn. 'Hi, I'm a Pegasus,' she made the Pegasus say.

There was a long pause.

'What happens now?' Izzy asked.

'You need a story,' I said. 'Maybe make them go somewhere.'

'Go where?' she asked.

'To . . . MAGIC MOUNTAIN,' I said.

Izzy blinked fast.

'Is that a real place?' she finally asked.

Izzy is *terrible* at playing **pretend**! I'd never tell her, though.

I put my Sweet Sisters dolls on my doona.

'Let's make this Magic Mountain,' I said, pointing to my bed. 'The Filly Friends want to take back their home from the EVIL GOBLIN QUEEN. The goblin queen is furry and grey.' I nudged Zeus with my foot. 'And these are her evil goblin servants.' I pointed to the Sweet Sisters. 'Maybe they have magic powers.'

'You can't **eat** the goblins,' Izzy told Zeus, who jumped onto the bed and was pawing at a Sweet Sister doll. 'They're your servants.'

'You take the goblins,' I told Izzy. 'I'll be the horses.'

And we played and we played until Dad told us it was time for bed.

MOST FUN EVER!

Stay tuned for more

THE TOP SECRET DIARIES OF TWIN SISTERS

TWINNING

in

FRIENDSHIP FALLOUT

Coming soon.